THE SEED

Written By Carissa Selena   Illustrated by Tori Meyer

One day, there was a tiny, little seed preparing for a very big adventure.

"Today is the day!" She shouted bouncing from leaf to leaf.

"Today is the day I see the world."

The tiny, little seed said goodbye to her family and friends,
took a deep breath, and jumped!

She smiled as she flew through the fresh, cool air.

She saw things she had never seen ...

fields of flowers,

glistening streams,

magnificent mountains,

and odd looking things.

She enjoyed flying from side to side,
going wherever the breeze took her.

After a while, it began to rain. At first, it felt nice because the tiny, little seed was hot.

Then, all of a sudden, the breeze turned into a gust and knocked the tiny, little seed off her path.

The wind grew stronger and the raindrops grew larger.

The sun was going down and the air was growing cold.

The tiny, little seed was scared.

A truck sped by, covering her in mud.
She could not see.

Exhausted, she decided to find a place
to rest for the night.

"Tomorrow is a new day," the tiny, little seed said to herself as she fell asleep.

That night, she had a wonderful dream of all the places she had yet to see.

She saw sunsets and rainbows, animals, and bugs. She saw stars and snow...

And then, she woke up.

The tiny, little seed breathed in the fresh air of a new day and took a big leap up toward the sky!

But something stopped her. She tried again, but the tiny, little seed was stuck.

She started to cry.

"Oh no!" She sobbed. "I have not seen everything I want to see!"

She took a few deep breaths and sat for a while, thinking about what she could do.

"I have a choice," the tiny, little seed said with determination.

As days went by, the tiny, little seed kept her face toward the sun.

SOME DAYS WERE **LOUD**...

Other days were quiet.

Some days she felt happy ...

and others were really tough.

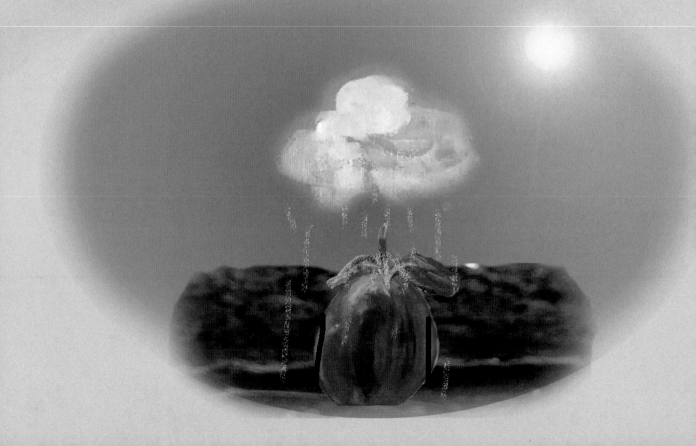

Some days she grew impatient.

Other days she enjoyed the ride.

Some days were full of company,

while other days were lonely.

And everything she felt was okay.

The tiny, little seed kept holding
onto her dreams.

Taking one day at a time, she kept growing.

With every inch, her hope would soar as she reached new heights.

Then, one day, something happened that proved to the tiny, little seed that everything she had been through was worth it.

You see, the tiny, little seed was not so tiny anymore. She had grown into a mighty, tall tree.

She took a moment to look at everything around her.

The mighty, tall tree had busted through that tiny crack and grown so tall she could finally see ...

fields of flowers,

glistening streams,

magnificent mountains,

and odd looking things.

Her place never changed.

Her outlook did.

The mighty, tall tree had the best view.

She kept on growing and so can you.

Photo by @mandypennphotography

Carissa believes the best teacher in her life has been transforming her hard experiences into beautiful gardens. She walks alongside others in hopes they will understand they are not alone and have the power to build extraordinary lives.

Carissa invites individuals to face their challenges in an honest and authentic way to heal and live the best lives possible. She believes that we are powerful beyond measure, and we all have the choice to light an ever-burning fire in ourselves.

Follow her at @theseedgrows

Photo by @ pure_images_studio

Tori Meyer is an illustrator who brings authors' words to life through her fine art. In addition to illustrating books, Tori also enjoys sharing her love of the West through her paintings and drawings.

She is a member of the Society of Children's Book Writers and Illustrators, and is a CIPA Award winner for her book, Journey Home, A Thank You To American Veterans. She lives in Parker, Colorado with her three daughters and their cat Lucky.

Follow her at www.torimeyer.com and Instagram @tori_meyer_art